Barbie™
Fairytopia

Magic
of the
Rainbow

A Junior Novelization

Adapted by Judy Katschke
Based on the screenplay by Elise Allen

SCHOLASTIC INC.

New York   Toronto   London   Auckland   Sydney
Mexico City   New Delhi   Hong Kong   Buenos Aires

ISBN-13: 978-0-439-88859-2
ISBN-10: 0-439-88859-X

BARBIE, FAIRYTOPIA, MERMAIDIA and associated trademarks and trade dress are owned by, and used under license from Mattel, Inc. © 2007 Mattel, Inc. All Rights Reserved.

Special thanks to Rob Hudnut, Tiffany J. Shuttleworth, Vicki Jaeger, Monica Okazaki, Luke Carroll, Cherish Bryck, Anita Lee, Kelly Shin, Pam Prostarr, Dave Lee, James Wallace, Tricia Jellis, Aeron Kline, Zoe Evamy, Steve Lumley, Shaun Martens, Lil Reichmann, Derek Toye, Sheila Turner, Eric Cheung, Peter Donnelly, Behzad Mansoori-Dara, Joel Olmstead, Craig Shiells, and Walter Martishius.

Published by Scholastic Inc.
SCHOLASTIC and associated logos are trademarks and/or registered trademarks of Scholastic Inc.

12 11 10 9 8 7 6 5 4 3 2 1   7 8 9 10 11/0

Printed in the U.S.A.
First printing, February 2007
Designed by Angela Jun

Chapter 1
A Surprise Visit

"Look!"

"Is that Elina?"

"It *is* Elina!"

Five excited pixies popped up from a flower bed as their fairy idol flew by. The pixies were tiny in size, but when it came to Elina, they were her *biggest* fans!

In a flash, the pixies shot off after Elina and her best friend, Dandelion. The fairies' delicate wings fluttered so fast, they were almost a blur.

Elina didn't see the trail of pixies behind

her. But she *did* see her blue puffball, Bibble, napping in the Magic Meadow below. With a twinkle in her rainbow-colored eyes, Elina swooped over Bibble, waking him with a start!

"*Bleep, blurple, bleeeee!*" Bibble shouted in surprise.

Bibble floated after Elina and Dandelion as they glided over Fairytopia, the most magical place beyond the rainbow. Shaped like a flower, the land was ruled by the loving Enchantress and her Guardian Fairies, one from each of Fairytopia's seven lands.

To Elina, Fairytopia was as beautiful as it was magical. Its rivers sparkled like diamonds. The air was always filled with the perfume of flowers. But today, the air was filled with the giggles of starstruck pixies.

"*Waaaa!*" Bibble shouted when he saw the flying fan club.

"What is it, Bibble?" Elina asked.

She whirled around and saw for herself —
a flock of wide-eyed pixies staring back
at her!

"Is it true you gave up your wings to save
Fairytopia?" one pixie asked.

"I heard that you fought off thirty Fungi
at once," another pixie said. "All by
yourself!"

"What?" Elina said. "No, I —"

"You're my hero," the tiniest pixie gushed. "Will you tell us all about the two times you saved Fairytopia?"

Dandelion and Bibble traded worried looks. Sure, they loved hearing about Elina earning her wings for fighting off Laverna, the Enchantress's evil twin sister. And about Elina tricking Laverna into eating the True Self Berry that turned the fairy witch into a warty toad. They loved hearing both stories — but not for the hundredth time!

Dandelion pulled Elina aside. "This happens all the time," she whispered. "You're just one fairy!"

Elina stared at Dandelion. True, she was still a fairy. But to the pixies, she was more. She was a hero!

"I know I'm the same fairy I've always been, but . . . everyone expects so much more of me now," Elina whispered back.

"I don't want to let them down."

Dandelion nodded. She didn't exactly agree. But she did understand.

"Okay," Elina told the pixies. "It all started when —"

"I hate to interrupt," a voice cut in. "But do you have a moment for an old friend?"

Elina looked up and smiled. She would know that gentle voice anywhere. It was Azura, one of the Guardian Fairies.

"Azura!" Elina exclaimed.

"*Bublurrra!*" Bibble chortled happily.

"I'm sorry, but I'm going to have to steal Elina away for now," Azura said with a smile. The disappointed pixies turned away. Elina's stories would have to wait.

"Do you think Peony will have us over for tea?" Azura asked Elina. "There's something we need to discuss."

Elina's knees grew weak. There was

something in Azura's tone that spelled trouble. And to most fairies, trouble was spelled L-A-V-E-R-N-A!

"It's Laverna, isn't it?" Elina asked, her voice trembling. "She's back and she's coming after me?"

"No, Elina," Azura said, surprised. "Is that what you're afraid of?"

"A little," Elina admitted. "Laverna can't be happy that I keep getting in her way. And if she really ate that True Self Berry . . ."

Elina shuddered at the thought. But Azura flashed a reassuring smile.

"Don't worry," Azura said. "Where Laverna is now, she can't hurt a fly."

But way below in the Magic Meadow, a Fungus named Max watched their every move. Max was Laverna's Head Fungus. He was also her spy!

"Will you be joining us, Dandelion?" Azura asked.

"I can't," Dandelion said. "I promised my mom I'd be home for dinner."

Elina said good-bye to her best friend. Then she, Azura, and Bibble flew off for the sweet-smelling petals of Peony.

Laverna's voice crackled through Max's magic medallion, making him jump. Laverna was in the Bogs of the Hinterland, but with the medallion she was just a scream away.

"Can't even hurt a fly!" Laverna sneered. "Is that some kind of joke?"

Laverna's toad face filled the screen on Max's medallion. He could see his mistress was hopping mad.

Jutting out her long tongue, Laverna flicked a fly into her gaping mouth. Gulping, she caught a glimpse of Max through his magic medallion.

"What are you looking at?" Laverna demanded. "Your job is to follow Azura!"

"Yes, Your Wartiness!" Max blurted. He clicked off his medallion and shot off.

Laverna's toady eyes bulged with delight as she imagined ruling Fairytopia. The fair Elina had destroyed her plans twice. But this time it would be different.

Chapter 2
A Challenge for Elina

"So this is Peony," Azura said. "She is absolutely lovely."

Peony's soft wall of petals began to quiver.

"She says thank you," Elina said. She knew Peony inside and out. That's because Peony was not just Elina's friend — she was her home.

Inside, Peony's pink petals formed everything from Elina's downy bed to a flowery dressing table. That day her petals shaped the tea table — even the pot of tea.

"So," Elina said, placing a plate of sweet cakes on the table. "You said there's something we need to discuss?"

"Yes," Azura said. "I want you to be my apprentice and learn to perform the Flight of Spring."

Bibble's mouth watered as he eyeballed the sweets. His mind wasn't on the Flight of Spring — it was on springing for the yummiest-looking sweet cake.

Elina listened while Azura continued, "Each year the Guardians gather to return spring to Fairytopia. If they fail, the land will be plunged into ten years of winter so bitter that nothing will survive."

"That's why it's so important to train apprentices," Azura added.

Bibble reached for a sweet cake and took a bite. The chomp hardly made a dent, but it did loosen his front tooth.

"*Bleepeeeee!!*" Bibble cheered.

Elina and Azura turned to Bibble. The little puffball was hovering over the table, wiggling his front tooth with his tongue!

"You have a loose tooth!" Elina exclaimed.

With a wink, Azura said, "Looks like someone will be getting a visit from my friend the Tooth Fairy!"

But Bibble had bigger plans. He told Elina and Azura that he planned to stay awake all night. That way he could catch the famous Tooth Fairy in the act!

"You can't catch the Tooth Fairy," Elina chuckled. "She never lets anyone see her!"

"Almost never," Azura said. "But your first tooth is a special occasion and deserves a gift."

Casting a spell, Azura created a tiny satin pouch for Bibble. It was to hold his tooth until the Tooth Fairy arrived.

"I'll see both of you at the Crystal Palace in two days," Azura said as she stood up to leave. "That's where you'll begin your classes and learn the Flight of Spring."

Too excited to speak, Elina waved as Azura flew off. In just two days she would learn the Flight of Spring!

"This is amazing, Bibble!" Elina shouted as she twirled her puffball around and around. "I have to tell Dandelion!"

Elina zipped off to find her best friend.

Bibble lagged behind, playfully wiggling

his loose tooth. As the puffball flitted around a corner, he spotted a colorful bed of flowers. Bibble sniffed the first flower. Lovely! He sniffed the second flower. Heavenly! But when Bibble sniffed the third flower . . . Stinky!

"*Phhleeeew!*" Bibble gagged.

Wearing a silly disguise of petals, Max waited until Bibble flew away. Then he quickly pulled out his medallion and called Laverna.

"That *is* interesting!" Laverna said upon hearing of Elina's apprenticeship. "From now on, I want you to follow Elina, not Azura!"

Chapter 3
Friends in the Forest

"Bibble, look!" Elina gasped.

It had been two days since Azura's visit. After flying over the Magic Meadow and through the Bluebell Forest, Elina and Bibble reached the Rustic Forest. Up ahead was the most amazing view of the Crystal Palace.

Bibble whistled past his loose tooth. The palace glistened in the late golden sun.

"Bibble," Elina said slowly, "what if I can't do this?"

"*Blllluuuh?*" Bibble chirped, confused.

Elina had saved Fairytopia from the evil Laverna twice. Anything after that would be a piece of sweet cake!

"Each Guardian chose one apprentice," Elina went on. "That's seven fairies out of all of Fairytopia. What if I'm not good enough?"

As Bibble opened his mouth to speak —

"It's okay, little one," a voice said. "Come along."

"Bibble?" Elina said, turning around. "Was that you?"

Bibble shook his head. The voice seemed to be coming from a small grove of fruit trees. Curious, Bibble took off to check it out.

"Bibble, wait!" Elina called.

Bibble popped his head between two fruit trees. Elina caught up and popped her head next to his.

"It's not nice to spy. Come on —" Elina

15

whispered softly to Bibble. But as she looked into the clearing, she saw a handsome boy kneeling by a river. He had a small horselike creature with him. Elina thought the horse was the cutest little thing she ever saw. So did Bibble as he sighed out loud.

"Shhh!" Elina warned.

But it was too late. The startled horse had already begun to neigh and rear up!

"I'm sorry," Elina said as she flew into the clearing. "We shouldn't even be here."

"We?" the boy asked.

Elina looked around for Bibble. Where did he go?

"My puffball," Elina explained. "I guess he already left."

The boy introduced himself. His name was Linden and the creature was a Tumby.

"She likes you," Linden said.

"How do you know?" Elina asked.

"I'm an Oread," Linden explained. "We're known for being good at languages."

Before Linden could say another word, Bibble raced out of the trees. In his hands was a half-eaten fruit!

Elina smiled as Bibble shared the fruit with the Tumby. She was glad her puffball had found a new friend.

"Are you Elina, Azura's apprentice?" Linden asked.

"Yes!" Elina replied. "Do Oreads read minds, too?"

"No," Linden chuckled. "But you were the only apprentice who wasn't at the dorms."

"Are you an apprentice, too?" Elina asked.

He nodded. "My name is Linden."

"What are the other apprentices like?" Elina asked.

"It's hard to tell," Linden admitted. "Some of them were talking about you. Is it true that you were the one who saved the Guardians from Laverna?"

Elina felt herself blush. The last thing she wanted was star treatment. Especially from a fellow apprentice.

"It's not as big a deal as it sounds," Elina said.

"At least you know you belong here," Linden sighed. "I'm afraid Topaz is going to see me and realize she made a big mistake!"

"You are?" Elina asked, her eyes lighting up.

"You don't have to sound so happy about it!" Linden laughed.

"No!" Elina said. "It's just that I'm a little nervous, too."

Elina knew that she had found a friend. But her thoughts were quickly interrupted by the Tumby's neighs.

"She says it's late," Linden translated. "She needs to get home to her mother."

"It *is* late," Elina said. "I should get to the dorms and meet everyone."

Linden offered to go with Elina. She shook her head politely and said, "I have to be strong. Azura expects that of me."

After saying good-bye to Linden, Elina and Bibble took off for the Crystal Palace.

As Elina and Bibble soared across the darkening sky, she did not see Max spying on them. Her eyes were set on the dorms up ahead — they dangled from tree branches like glowing ornaments!

"I wonder which one is ours," Elina said. "What do you think, Bibble . . . Bibble?"

Elina turned to see Bibble rocketing straight for the dorms. But just as he zoomed into a doorway, Elina grabbed him back.

"Bibble!" Elina scolded. "You can't just fly in here. We don't know if it's ours!"

"News flash," a voice said. "It *isn't*!"

Chapter 4
Laverna's Spy

Glancing into the room, Elina thought she was dreaming. The room looked like a vision of the night sky. There were moons and stars everywhere.

Two fairies were sitting across from each other on a bed. One fairy was pinkish orange and had giant pigtails. The other was a blue-violet color with wings shaped like half-moons. Her eyes were closed as if she were deep in thought.

"I'm Elina and this is Bibble," Elina said with a smile. "And . . . you are?"

"Not interested in having uninvited guests," the smaller fairy said meanly.

"Shimmer!" the blue-violet fairy cried. Her eyes snapped wide open. "I see something!"

She looked straight at Elina and said, "I see terror . . . tragedy . . . doom!"

Then she flashed a perky smile and said, "I'm Lumina. Pleased to meet you!"

Lumina was a moon fairy, able to read the future.

"I came in here to have *my* future read," Shimmer shouted at Elina and Bibble. "Now get out!"

"Maybe we should try another room," Elina decided.

The next room was as strange as the first. This one was covered with mirrors and occupied by a Merrow named Faben.

"I was hoping you could help me," Elina said.

"You were looking for my autograph, right?" Faben asked with a gleaming smile. "A picture of Fairytopia's lead apprentice?"

Elina shot Bibble a sideways glance. Faben was clearly in love with himself. And they were clearly in the wrong room!

Elina and Bibble made their way to the next room. This room was splashed in hot shades of orange and red. Everything inside shone as if lit by the sun.

Elina shaded her eyes with her hand as she looked around the room. Catching rays in the middle was Sunburst. Sunburst was a sparkle fairy.

"Excuse me," Elina said. "I —"

Sunburst peeked over her sunshades. "You must be Elina," she said.

Elina smiled with relief. At last — a friendly apprentice! But Elina's hopes were crushed when Sunburst snapped, "I was hoping you wouldn't show!"

"What?" Elina gasped.

"Let's get something clear," Sunburst said. "I don't care about your whole 'I saved Fairytopia and everybody should bow down to me —'"

"I never said that!" Elina protested.

Sunburst held up her sparkly palm like a fairy crossing guard. "Talk to the sparkle," she said. "I think you should leave now!"

Elina shook her head as she and Bibble left the room. How could anybody so sunny be . . . so cold?

"Don't let her bother you," a voice piped up. "I don't think she's a very nice fairy."

Elina spun around. Standing at the next room was a sweet-looking wood nymph.

"I'm Elina," Elina said.

"I'm Glee," the fairy said. Her eyes instantly lit up when she spotted Bibble.

"Is that your puffball?"

"Yes," Elina said. "This is Bibble. He —"

Before Elina could finish, Glee yanked Bibble through the door. When Elina flew into the room, she thought she was inside a forest — everything there was made out of twigs, vines, bushes, and leaves!

"Bibble," Glee said with a sweep of her arm. "Meet Dizzle!"

Elina saw another puffball, lounging on a small vine-covered bed. Unlike Bibble, this puffball was pink. And very beautiful!

"*Ooooh!*" Bibble swooned.

"I think he likes her," Glee whispered.

Dizzle's lashes fluttered as she smiled shyly at Bibble. But when she spotted his loose tooth, she zoomed over, almost knocking him down.

The puffballs chattered about Bibble's loose tooth and about meeting the Tooth Fairy. While they got to know each other, Elina got to know Glee.

"Your room is beautiful," Elina said.

"Thanks," Glee said. "The Guardians decorated rooms for their apprentices to make them feel at home. How do you like your room?"

"I haven't seen it yet," Elina answered.

"Come on. I'll show you," Glee said as she led Elina to her room.

Walking inside, Elina smiled. The room looked exactly like Peony!

"It does feel like home!" Elina sighed.

The soft tinkling of bells filled the air. Peeking outside, Elina saw several bluebells ringing out a gentle lullaby.

"See you in the morning," Glee said with a yawn.

"First day of classes," Elina added.

"I know," Glee said. "I'm a little nervous, but you're probably not. After everything you've done, this has to be nothing for you!"

Elina opened her mouth to disagree but Glee had already left the room. If only the other apprentices knew how nervous she really was!

The bluebells tolled as the apprentices got ready for bed. Way down below the dorms, Max was already tucked in for the night.

"And that's everything," Max reported into his medallion. "She met a boy who speaks a little animal. Swapped chitchat

27

with a bunch of fairies, then went to bed. Total sum of usefulness? Zippo!"

"You think so?" Laverna snapped on the other end. "Because what I just heard was the perfect opening to get me on the throne of Fairytopia!"

Laverna ordered Max back to the bogs. He had to carry out her sinister new plan!

"Ah, sister," Laverna said as she snapped her own medallion shut. "How appropriate that you've made your palace a school. Because soon all of Fairytopia will learn a lesson they'll never forget!"

Chapter 5
First Day of School

Seven excited apprentices stood outside of the dorms. Elina and Glee traded smiles as the Guardians arrived. This was it — the big day!

"Welcome, apprentices and honored puffball guests," Azura announced.

Bibble and Dizzle puffed their chests out proudly.

"You have been invited to the Crystal Palace to learn from the Guardians how to perform the Flight of Spring," Azura went on. "This annual ritual releases a magical rainbow that gives Fairytopia another year of vitality."

All the apprentices watched and listened carefully as Azura conjured a hologram to illustrate what she was talking about.

"First, we use Magic to extract light from water, creating the chamber where the ceremony takes place." As Azura spoke, the hologram showed beautiful rainbow lights arcing from the water to create a dome.

"Then we perform the art of Flance: the combination of flight and dance, which draws the blush from the inner fountain." With a wave of her hand, Azura changed the hologram to show beautiful dancing fairies.

"Finally, through Luminescence, we channel our light energy into the blush, releasing the first rainbow of spring. If the ceremony is done correctly, Fairytopia will flourish." Azura stopped and took a deep breath. "If not, the blush will wither and our land will be doomed to a ten-year bitter winter."

Magically, scrolls appeared in each apprentice's hands. "These are your class schedules. I look forward to seeing you in class. Good luck."

Glee leaned over toward Elina. "I have Magic first. You?"

"Same!" Elina smiled and the two girls hugged with joy.

Bibble and Dizzle were also glad they would be together.

"Welcome to Magic class," Tourmaline announced that morning. "Each of you has a unique strength that allows you to use Magic. Focus this energy to visualize the separation of light from water." Tourmaline demonstrated by creating a beautiful wave

of multicolored light. Then he paused and looked at each of his students. "Sunburst, please demonstrate."

Sunburst stepped forward and repeated exactly what Tourmaline had done.

"Very impressive, Sunburst," Tourmaline said proudly. "I think we know someone who will have *no* problems handling the Flight of Spring."

"Elina, what can you do?" Tourmaline asked.

Elina stepped forward. Her rainbow eyes glimmered as she concentrated. Then a blue light shot from her hands, creating the most stunning waterfall!

Elina didn't know how she did it. She just knew everyone in the class was impressed. Everyone except Sunburst.

"Cut it out, Elina!" Sunburst cried as the wave of magical water came closer to her. "When sparkle fairies touch water, we lose all of our power. As if you didn't know that!"

"I didn't know!" Elina exclaimed. The river of light became bigger and bigger, and Sunburst backed away.

With a flick of his wrist, Tourmaline made the waterfall disappear. "Pretty impressive, Elina," Tourmaline said, "but you need to learn to control your powers." He turned to Sunburst. "Looks like you have some competition for best in class."

Elina caught Sunburst's icy glare. The last thing she wanted was an enemy!

✽ ✽ ✽

"Welcome to your first lesson in Flance," Topaz said later that afternoon. "Through flight and dance you will learn to work together to draw the blush from the inner fountain. I will demonstrate." Soft music began to play and Topaz spun through the air, landing on brightly colored gems. She had the grace of a prima ballerina.

"Now you'll each give it a try." Topaz turned to Elina. "How about you go first, Elina?"

Her stomach did a triple flip as all eyes fell upon her. She let herself feel the music and then took a deep breath. As the gems appeared in the sky, Elina landed on them one by one.

When the song ended, Elina turned to Topaz. The Guardian's mouth hung wide open.

"Was it that horrible?" Elina asked.

"Horrible?" Topaz exclaimed. "Elina, that was incredible!"

Elina was too surprised to speak. She had aced Flance!

"Show-off," Faben muttered.

"Tell me about it!" said Sunburst in a huff.

Chapter 6
Witchy, Wicked, and Warty

Meanwhile, in the Bogs of the Hinterland, Elina's biggest enemy was hatching a plan.

"Finally!" Laverna said. "I can leave these dreaded bogs and put my plan into action!"

"If you leave without a royal pardon from the Enchantress," Max reminded, "you'll become a *real* toad."

"I'll be a real toad when I leave," Laverna agreed. "But only until a fairy spell releases me!"

Max stared at Laverna. Did he get

swamp water in his ears? Or did he just hear what he thought he heard?

"But what fairy would want to release you?" Max asked slowly.

A smile spread across Laverna's warty face. She already had one fairy in mind.

"Welcome to Luminescence," Azura said proudly later that evening. "Each one of you has a powerful energy inside of you, one that can be thrown into the world as a brilliant magical light." Azura demonstrated by creating a shimmering ball of golden light. "If you want to learn how to coax open the First Blush of Spring, you'll need to focus your light energy."

Azura looked at her students. "Elina. Sunburst. Why don't you try casting your inner light on this flower?"

Elina focused, but nothing happened.

Sunburst laughed a little, but that made Elina try even harder. Now, instead of focusing her energy on the flower, Elina mistakenly focused it on Sunburst. Now Sunburst was blue!

"How dare you!" Sunburst shrieked.

"It was an accident," Elina said.

Sunburst didn't believe Elina. She narrowed her eyes and cast a spell in Elina's direction.

"No!" Elina cried, but it was too late. Now Elina was orange!

Elina immediately fired back with a spell that turned Sunburst a pink plaid.

"Enough!" shouted an angry Azura. *"Annullsera-Revelsera-Expungerillimmersera-Nulliferous, Null!"* Instantly, both girls were back to normal.

"I never want to catch anyone using Magic on another apprentice ever again. Is that clear?" Azura added.

Elina and Sunburst knew Azura meant business.

"Yes, Azura," they said together.

Chapter 7
Elina's Mistake

The Rustic Forest was peaceful. The lightning-bug fairies filled the trees with twinkling lights. Elina wished she could enjoy the scene as she strolled with Linden. But she was too worried to enjoy anything.

"Maybe Azura made a mistake," Elina said. "Maybe I just don't belong here."

"You're the most talented apprentice here!" Linden insisted. "Talk to Azura about it. I'm sure she'd make you feel better."

"I would never!" Elina said, shaking her

head. "It would make me seem weak."

Elina explained how the fairies expected her to be their strong, confident hero. If she didn't act that way, she would let them down.

"It's better to be strong and not disappoint anyone," Elina sighed.

They heard a rustling noise and turned around. A few feet away was a toad, limping slowly toward them.

"Poor thing," Elina said. "Is it okay?"

"I can speak a little Toad," Linden said. "I'll find out."

Linden and the toad croaked back and forth. Elina still couldn't believe Linden could talk with animals!

"She says she's from the Bogs of the Hinterlands," Linden translated. "She's been cursed by an exiled fairy witch."

"By Laverna!" Elina gasped. "What other exiled fairy witches are in the bogs?"

Linden listened as the toad croaked on.

"She says the curse can only be broken by a fairy undoing the spell," Linden added.

Elina and Linden thought hard. Did they ever learn an undoing spell in class? After a while, Elina's eyes lit up.

"I think I know one!" Elina said as she repeated the spell that Azura had used earlier: "*Annullsera-Revelsera-Expungerillimmersera-Nulliferous, Null!*"

A burst of magic surrounded the toad. When the light was gone, so was the toad.

In its place was —

"Laverna!" Elina gasped.

"That's right, darling," Laverna said with a sly smile. "Did you miss me?"

"Elina, I don't understand," Linden said. "You turned the toad into . . . Laverna?"

"No, that *is* Laverna!" Elina said in disbelief.

"You have just sealed Fairytopia's fate!" Laverna cackled. "Pleasant dreams!"

Stunned, Elina and Linden watched as the evil fairy shot into the sky.

"Elina," Linden said slowly. "Did . . . we . . . just . . .?"

"*I* just," Elina groaned. "I just released Laverna to destroy Fairytopia."

Elina and Linden flew off to warn the Guardians.

When they reached the Guardians'

Lounge, Elina opened the door a crack. She called carefully through the door, "Um . . . hello?"

Tourmaline barely looked up from his reading. "Apprentices aren't allowed in the Guardians' Lounge," he said.

"Then there's probably a good reason they're here," Azura said, waving Elina and Linden inside. "How can we help you?"

Elina gathered her courage, then she told the Guardians the whole story. When Elina was finished, she waited for the worst. Would she be expelled from school? Banished from the Crystal Palace?

After an uncomfortable moment of silence, Tourmaline threw back his head and laughed.

"What's so funny?" Linden asked.

"That you've been fooled by Laverna," Tourmaline said. "Laverna learned about the apprentices, then used a spell to make you believe you released her."

"Why would she do that?" Azura asked.

"To get us all in a panic when we should be thinking about the Flight of Spring!" Tourmaline said.

To prove his point, Tourmaline led everyone to the Guardian Glass. An image of the bogs appeared in the magic mirror. There, being fanned by two Fungi — was a toad!

"Laverna does seem to be there," Azura admitted.

"But I know Laverna," Elina said. "And it was she!"

Azura took Elina's news seriously. She promised to increase security at the Crystal Palace — just in case.

"You can head back to your rooms," Azura said. "We'll take it from here."

As Elina and Linden left, the image in the mirror began to fade. But the toad in the

Bogs of the Hinterland continued to be fanned.

"Hey, Max!" an exhausted Fungus said. "How long do you have to make us work like this?"

"Don't complain until you've had to trade your beautiful body for that of a toad!" Max said.

Elina had been right all along. The toad in the Guardian Glass was a fake. And the *real* Laverna was only a hop, skip, and jump away!

Chapter 8
Sunburst's Secret

"I'm afraid to face everyone," Elina told Linden. They were just nearing the dorms when Glee, Bibble, and Dizzle charged toward them.

"*Bleepppaaaplllibbblebooppleelelele,*" Bibble babbled like a runaway fairy train.

"You're talking too fast," Elina said. "I don't understand!"

"You'd talk fast, too, if you just lost your tooth!" Glee said with a smile.

Bibble held up his tooth proudly and placed it into the special pouch that

Azura had given him.

As the puffballs flew away to try to meet the Tooth Fairy, Glee studied Elina and Linden.

"You both look so sad," Glee said.

Before Elina could explain, they were joined by their classmates.

"Shouldn't you resign after what you did?" Faben asked Elina.

"What?" Glee asked in confusion.

"Elina released Laverna," Faben explained. "And right before the Flight of Spring!"

"It was an accident!" Elina said.

"It was treason!" Shimmer snapped.

"I'm sensing a dark cloud of blackness in your future," Lumina told Elina.

Lumina, Faben, and Shimmer winged away. But Sunburst stayed with Elina.

"I'm sorry," Sunburst said. "I'm sure you didn't mean for this to happen."

Elina watched with amazement as Sunburst flew away. The sparkle fairy had never been this kind to her!

"I guess disaster brings out the best in her," Linden said in surprise.

"What do we do now?" Glee asked.

"I don't know," Elina said. "But I can't let Laverna ruin the Flight of Spring!"

Laverna's plan was already in motion. With her evil magic, she had taken over the shape and voice of Sunburst. Soon she would take over the Flight of Spring — and all of Fairytopia!

"Don't you just love the way the colors fly off my fingers?" Laverna said to herself in Sunburst's room later that day. She grinned as she flicked orange sparkles from her fingertips. "I always wanted to be a sparkle fairy!"

That evening, Azura made an announcement: "Due to recent events, all apprentices and Guardians will take turns patrolling the Crystal Palace. Tonight Elina and Sunburst will patrol with Tourmaline."

"Extra work for us," Shimmer huffed. "Thanks a lot, Elina."

"It won't be so bad," Sunburst said cheerily. "See you tonight!"

As they flew off, the other apprentices eyed Sunburst.

Since when was *she* so cheerful?

But the last person to be cheerful that day was Elina. She still felt very bad about her mistake.

Elina sighed and flew to her room to check on Bibble. There she found both puffballs with the tooth pouch. They were snoring!

"Bibble?" Elina whispered. "Dizzle?"

"*Waaaaa!*" the puffballs cried as they snapped awake. Did they miss the Tooth Fairy?

Bibble dug into his pouch and sighed with relief. His tooth was still there!

"You should get some sleep," Elina said. "I'll be on patrol for Laverna, but —"

Elina stopped midsentence when she spotted an envelope on her bed. She opened the envelope and pulled out a letter.

Bibble and Dizzle listened while Elina read it out loud: "'The time has come to face me one-on-one. Meet me in the Rustic Forest. I will be waiting. Laverna.'"

The puffballs chirped frantically. They tried to convince Elina to let them come along.

"I started this by letting her out," Elina said. "It's up to me to finish it. I'm going alone."

Elina hugged Bibble and Dizzle good-bye. Then she made her way into the Rustic Forest — alone!

❋ ⋆ ❋ ⋆ ❋

"I know you're out here, Laverna," Elina shouted in the dark. "Show yourself!"

A voice called Elina's name.

But it was not Laverna's.

"Linden!" Elina said as her friend came into view. "You have to go back. It's not safe for you here."

"Something happened to Azura," Linden said. "Come with me."

Linden led Elina to the Guardians' Lounge.

Inside she saw Sunburst holding a cool aloe plant to her bruised forehead. Dizzle and Bibble were leaning over Azura, who was unconscious.

"No!" Elina cried.

"She's alive," Glee assured her.

"Azura was poisoned by a rare toad venom," Linden explained. "It can only be found in a toad known to the Bogs of the Hinterland."

"So Laverna poisoned Azura!" Elina gasped.

Elina felt a pang of guilt. Was this her fault?

"And all the other Guardians," Shimmer said, walking in with the other apprentices. "We looked for another Guardian to help but they're in the same shape as Azura."

"Will they be okay?" Elina asked.

"Eventually," Linden said. "It can only wear off with time."

The apprentices exchanged worried looks.

"With the Guardians unconscious," Faben said, "who will perform the Flight of Spring?"

"No one," Lumina said. "I see it now. The Flight of Spring will not happen — and all of Fairytopia is *doomed*!"

And it's all my fault, Elina thought.

"Isn't it perfect, Maxie?" Laverna asked later that day.

Max looked at her through the magic medallion, licking his dry froggy lips. "Who knew you'd need so much toad spit to poison seven Guardians?" he croaked.

"Sunburst!" a voice called.

Laverna hid the medallion behind her back just before Faben poked his head into the room.

"The Enchantress wants to see all the apprentices about the Flight of Spring," Faben said.

"Wow!" Laverna said with a toss of her fiery hair. "I'll be right there!"

Laverna waited until Faben left. Then she grinned back into the medallion and said, "Don't you just love it when a plan comes together?"

"Yes," Max said. "Now about me still being a toad . . ."

"All in good time, my little Fungus," Laverna said. She straightened her sparkly fairy wings and smiled. "Right now I have an appointment with the Enchantress."

Chapter 9
Saving Spring

"I need you all to be brave and strong," the Enchantress said. "Without the Guardians, you have to perform the Flight of Spring."

All seven apprentices stood before the Enchantress. They couldn't believe what they were hearing.

"Us?" Shimmer gasped.

"We haven't trained enough!" Faben protested.

"I see very, very bad things happening if we try this!" Lumina predicted.

"I see bad things happening if you

don't," the Enchantress said. "We have one day to prepare. I will train you personally. Can I count on you?"

Elina stepped forward. This could be a way of making up for her mistakes.

"I'm in, too," Sunburst said cheerily. "If we try, I know we'll succeed!"

Everyone stared at Sunburst. It wasn't like the sparkle fairy to be so cheery. What was up with her?

Then, one by one, the other apprentices

stepped forward. They were nervous about performing the Flight of Spring but determined to try.

"Together we're strong!" said the Enchantress.

But training got off to a weak start. Lumina, Linden, and Shimmer turned Flance into a crash course as they accidentally ran into one another. Instead of creating a wall of light out of the water in Magic, Faben and Glee created an out-of-control wave!

Elina and Sunburst had better luck with Luminescence. Elina painted a lovely sunrise while Sunburst painted the perfect mountain. A little too perfect! Quickly Sunburst turned the mountain into a stinky lava-spewing volcano!

The Enchantress refused to give up as she coached late into the night. But would the apprentices be ready?

Trumpet flowers blared and bluebells tolled through the Crystal Palace. The apprentices gathered outside the palace, ready to perform the Flight of Spring!

"This is your moment, apprentices," the Enchantress told them. "Remember — Together we're strong!"

As they filed into the courtyard, Sunburst turned to Elina. "I know we'll both do great!" she said perkily.

Elina raised an eyebrow at Sunburst. Something about the sparkle fairy just didn't add up!

The Enchantress sat high above the courtyard on a throne. Behind her hovered the anxious Bibble and Dizzle.

The Enchantress clapped her hands three times. Together, the apprentices chanted their first magic spell.

Each apprentice concentrated on his or her river. They successfully changed their waters to red, orange, yellow, green, blue, indigo, and violet.

The rivers rose into a colored wall. Shaping the waters, the apprentices formed the Rainbow Dome. From the center of the dome a fountain rose. The waters parted to reveal the bud of the First Blush of Spring!

"*Wooooowwwwww!!*" Bibble and Dizzle exclaimed.

The apprentices then moved from their places to join their partners. Elina teamed up with Sunburst to begin Flance.

"I can't believe we're actually here," Elina said. "I think we can do this."

"Of course we can," Sunburst said. "You wouldn't let some limping toad get in your way, right?"

Elina stared at Sunburst. "How did you

know the toad limped?" she asked. "I never told anyone that!"

"Really?" Sunburst said with a smirk.

Elina looked deep into Sunburst's eyes. That's when it finally clicked. . . .

"You're not Sunburst!" Elina declared.

"Prove it," Sunburst snapped.

Elina's heart began to race.

In order to perform the Flight of Spring, she had to find Sunburst — the *real* Sunburst!

As Elina turned away, Linden flew over.

"Elina! Where are you going?" Linden asked.

In practically one breath, Elina explained everything to Linden.

"Sunburst isn't Sunburst — she's Laverna! I just need to get the *real* Sunburst back before Luminescence," Elina said, "when the blush starts to open!"

Elina shot out of the Rainbow Dome with Bibble and Dizzle not far behind. But as she flew over the Crystal Palace, she didn't see the real Sunburst anywhere at all.

"How am I going to find her?" Elina wondered.

Just then Sunburst's own words came to Elina's mind: *When sparkle fairies touch water, we lose all of our power!*

"That's it!" Elina said. "Laverna would have put Sunburst in water to take away her power!"

With little time to spare, Elina and the puffballs raced to the river in the Rustic Forest. A flash of orange underwater caught her eye.

Holding her breath, Elina dove into the water. The puffballs waited anxiously at the surface. For what seemed like an eternity, Elina swam toward a magic chamber holding Sunburst captive. Elina reached into the chamber and pulled Sunburst with all her might.

Sunburst was freed!

Elina helped Sunburst up to the surface

and onto dry land. The puffballs cheered in excitement.

"Elina?" Sunburst said in a weak voice. "Laverna . . . She —"

"I know everything," Elina said gently. Elina offered Sunburst a hand and helped her to her feet. "And it's worse than you think. Come on! We've got to get back to the Rainbow Dome."

The First Blush had begun to open when Elina and Sunburst burst into the Rainbow Dome.

"Hurry, Elina!" Linden cried. "It's time for Luminescence."

The First Blush started to open.

"No!" Elina cried. She pointed her finger at the sparkle fairy beside her. "*This* is the real Sunburst. That is *Laverna*!"

Chapter 10
Together and Strong

The fake Sunburst's eyes began to swirl. Laverna's wicked laughter filled the dome.

"Ta-da! Surprised?" Laverna sneered, as she turned back into her evil self.

The apprentices stood frozen with fear.

Laverna turned to the Enchantress as she pointed a threatening finger at the First Blush.

"Dear sister, make a move on me and I will destroy your First Blush of Spring. And all of your Fairytopia will be plunged into winter."

The Enchantress paled at the thought. How could she risk the future of Fairytopia? "Tell me what you want," she said.

With a wave of her hand, Laverna created a bubble. "I want you to step inside this spell chamber, where all your powers will be useless," she said. "And hand over the throne of Fairytopia to me!"

Elina gasped under her breath. This couldn't be happening!

"If I do what you say, you will spare the First Blush of Spring?" the Enchantress asked.

"Yes, sister, I will," Laverna replied. "Cross my heart."

The Enchantress bowed her head as the crown magically disappeared and reappeared on Laverna's brow.

Then she stepped inside the spell chamber.

Laverna laughed. "Did you really think

I'd save your people? Now watch as I destroy your precious First Blush of Spring!"

Laverna turned toward the First Blush and unleashed a black bolt of light. But Elina had to stop her. She jumped in front of the First Blush — and right into harm's way.

"Did you really think one little fairy like you could defeat me?" Laverna said.

Elina put up her hands, battling Laverna's dark magic with her own magical light. But Laverna was too strong, and Elina's magic was beginning to weaken.

It was then that the words of the Enchantress echoed through her head: *We're all in this together, and together we are strong.*

"I need you!" Elina shouted to the other apprentices.

"Your little apprentice friends can't help

you," Laverna sneered. "I'll pick them off one at a time."

Sunburst came to a quick realization. "We won't be coming for you one at a time," she said as she threw all her light toward Elina. The apprentices gathered together. Then, one by one, they threw their light and magic into Elina's wings.

The bright colors swirled inside Elina's wings, then burst out as a single rainbow, pushing Laverna's black ball of magic back toward her.

"Noooo!" Laverna cried. "I hate rainbows!"

The rainbow energy proved to be much stronger than the blackness and, with a blast, Laverna disappeared!

As the last traces of Laverna's magic frittered away, the Enchantress's spell chamber began to fade. But Elina, weak from her ordeal, struggled to get to her feet.

The apprentices rushed to Elina's side. Sunburst offered Elina a hand, and helped her to her feet.

"Thank you, all of you," Elina said gratefully.

"Elina — your wings!" Shimmer gasped.

Elina glanced over her shoulder. Her wings were much larger and sparkly. They were all the colors of the rainbow, too!

Elina gasped. "Look at the First Blush of Spring!"

Everyone turned toward the First Blush. It had totally wilted!

Then snow began to fall, even inside the chamber.

"Oh, that's it, then. Fairytopia is doomed!" Faben said with a groan.

"No, there's still life in the blush," Elina said. "We have to work together. It's our only chance to save it."

The apprentices formed a circle around the First Blush and focused their energy. As the energy built, it wrapped itself around the First Blush. As the healed blush began to open, it released the First Rainbow of Spring. The beautiful rainbow glowed throughout Fairytopia, waking the Guardians from their poisoned sleep.

"The First Blush is healed," the Enchantress declared. "And ready for next year's Flight of Spring!"

🦋 ✦ 🦋 ✦ 🦋

The apprentices and Guardians were gathered at the top of the Crystal Palace to hear the Enchantress's farewell address.

"Apprentices," the Enchantress began, "today you go back to your homes, but you don't return as the same fairies you once were."

"I thank you, and Fairytopia thanks you!" the Enchantress said at the end of her speech. With a wave of her hand, each of the apprentices received a special necklace.

The seven Guardians applauded the apprentices. Azura smiled at Elina as if to say, "Job well done!"

Bibble and Dizzle were watching the Enchantress so carefully that they did not notice as a little hand reached over and took the tooth pouch. It was quickly returned, but it no longer held Bibble's tooth. Instead, there was a sweet surprise inside.

As the pouch glistened with fairy sparkle it caught the puffballs' attention. They looked around to find the Tooth Fairy, but all that was left were a few sparkles.

The puffballs grabbed their prize and dashed to find Elina and Glee!

The apprentices gathered to say good-bye. Sunburst approached Elina and said, "I have a question. How did you know Lavern was doing the flight and not me?"

"Easy!" Elina said. "Laverna was nice to me!" They shared a laugh and hugged again.

Elina waved to her new lifelong friends as she soared away from the Crystal Palace and home toward the Magic Meadow. Her beautiful wings would always remind her of her friends and how they had worked together to save Fairytopia!